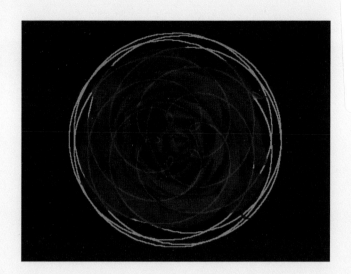

VENUS WISDOM CREDO

1. **Venus Wisdom** recognizes the wisdom of Venus as the golden key to actualizing the positive timeline in the Age of Aquarius.

2. **Venus Wisdom** honors Venus as a reflection of our care, our heart wisdom, and our ability to form bonds that create positive relationships.

3. **Venus Wisdom** uses Venus' 19-month dance with the Sun as the container for the energies and themes arising in the Sky Story.

4. **Venus Wisdom** prioritizes our human empowerment and the transformation of our hearts as we move through Venus' cycle.

5. **Venus Wisdom** engages with the Venus cycle as a living map to guide us on our heroine's journey; shedding what is false, fortifying our ability to connect with Source within, embody our truth, and live our sacred purpose.

6. **Venus Wisdom** teaches us how to sync with Venus through receiving her light, feeling her movements, and attuning to the New and Peak Venus Portals as doorways into our inner knowing.

7. **Venus Wisdom** reflects our own Feminine Essence back to us through our Venus Avatar; a glimpse of our infinite nature.

8. **Venus Wisdom** shows us how to anchor the Solar Feminine frequency on the planet to co-create a new reality in alignment with natures' principles.

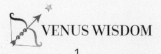

The Solar Feminine was birthed on the planet on June 3rd, 2012 when Venus visibly crossed the face of the Sun for the last time in our lifetime.

The Sun and Venus together are the union of Fire and Water, Eros and Heart, Light and Love, Source and Body.

A new cycle begins January 8, 2022, when Venus and Sun unite at 18° Capricorn and create a new Venus Star Point.

The Initiating, Feminine, Earth archetype of Capricorn will infuse the entire 19-month cycle.

Solar Feminine continues to be anchored as we move deeper into the Age of Aquarius. Uranus, the Great Awakener, in Venus' sign of Taurus until 2026 underlines the importance of Venus at this change of ages. In 2022, the North Node representing the north star of our collective evolution moves into Taurus, further emphasizing the power of Venus at this time. The revolution is IN. Great changes will come as we embody more love.

The Solar Feminine teaches us Heart-Centered Leadership; how to risk living in the present moment, how to stabilize in the unknown, consider all possibilities until we receive clarity, and then take the right action for us. We lead by trusting our heart's intelligence above all else.

In the Venus in Capricorn cycle, the sacred feminine takes her throne and puts on her crown. Here, she is the Queen of Integrity and enjoys the Pleasure of Manifesting. Her throne is her knowledge of the Earth's intelligence gained through her humbling to nature's principles. Her crown is her cosmic wisdom as an infinite being. She is us.

In this cycle, we are invited to learn the power of saying "NO" to what is not right, claim the full authority of our heart's wisdom and take responsibility for creating the world we want our grandchildren to live in. We are seeding the New Earth - a culture based on care, interconnection, reverence for life, and the natural world. Together, we will be initiated into the Capricorn Mysteries and discover our role in this Great Turning.

The monthly New Venus Portals (Moon-Venus conjunctions) are marked on the Venus Cycle map with their symbols, dates and the degree of the meeting. The New and Peak Venus Portals (Moon-Venus oppositions) are on the day in the calendar. The Key Dates on pages 30 & 32 feature the important dates for Venus in this cycle. In the calendar, stars mark the dates with key dates so you can refer to the Key Dates page to find out what is happening.

Join us in the Venus Wisdom Collective to receive guidance on how to sync with Venus to stay anchored in your heart, embody your deeper truth and manifest your greatest visions in these tumultuous times! We will be moving off FB in 2022 so be sure to join our email list.

Love,
Sasha Rose & the Venus Wisdom Team
www.venuswisdom.com

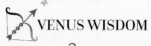

The Venus Cycle as the Heroine's Journey of Our Sacred Feminine

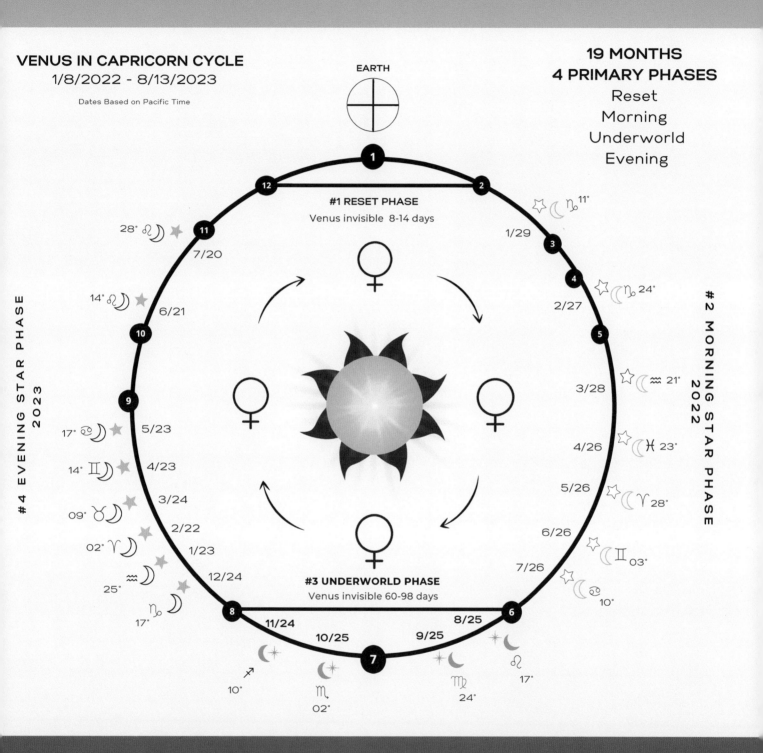

VENUS IN CAPRICORN CYCLE
1/8/2022 - 8/13/2023

Dates Based on Pacific Time

19 MONTHS
4 PRIMARY PHASES
Reset
Morning
Underworld
Evening

EARTH

#1 RESET PHASE
Venus invisible 8-14 days

#3 UNDERWORLD PHASE
Venus invisible 60-98 days

#2 MORNING STAR PHASE 2022

#4 EVENING STAR PHASE 2023

1/29 — ♑ 11°
2/27 — ♑ 24°
3/28 — ♒ 21°
4/26 — ♓ 23°
5/26 — ♈ 28°
6/26 — ♊ 03°
7/26 — ♋ 10°

8/25
9/25
10/25 — ♍ 24°
11/24 — ♏ 02°
10° ♐

8 — 17° ♑
25° ♒
02° ♈
09° ♉
14° ♊ 17° ♋ — 5/23
17° ♋
6/21 — 14° ♌
7/20 — 28° ♌

17° ♌
24° ♍

12/24
1/23
2/22
3/24
4/23

1	Venus Meets Sun Interior 1/8	4	Greatest Morn. Brilliance 2/9	7	Venus Meets Sun Ext. 10/22	10	Greatest Eve. Brilliance 7/10/23
2	Rises in East as Morn. Star 1/13	5	Morn Max Elongation 3/20	8	Rises as Evening Star 12/1	11	Venus Retrograde 7/22/23
3	Venus goes Direct 1/29	6	Sets in East- Morn. Star 8/14	9	Evening Max Elong. 6/4/23	12	Sets as Eve. Star 8/8/23

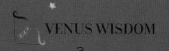

VENUS WISDOM

My Birth Chart

PRINT YOUR CHART AND PASTE OR TAPE HERE

You can print that for free at: www.astro.com

Encouraged to select Whole Sign House system

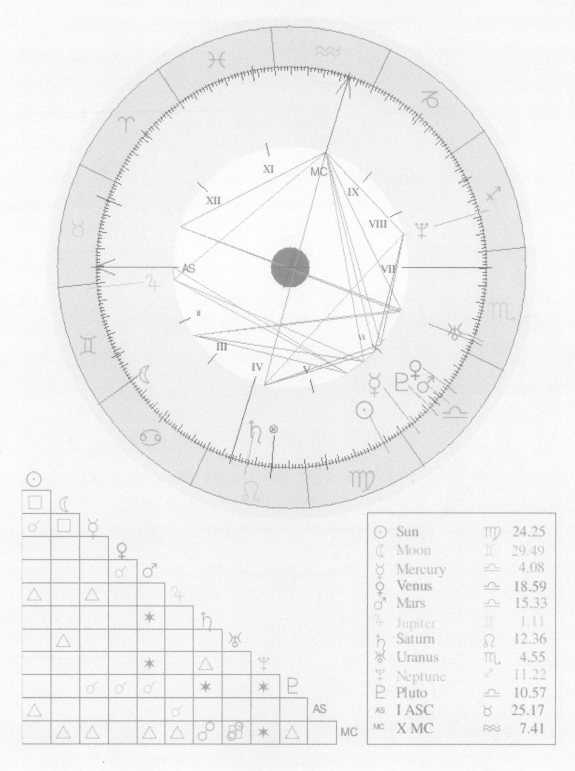

☉	Sun	♍	24.25
☽	Moon	♊	29.49
☿	Mercury	♎	4.08
♀	Venus	♎	18.59
♂	Mars	♎	15.33
♃	Jupiter	♊	1.11
♄	Saturn	♌	12.36
♅	Uranus	♏	4.55
♆	Neptune	♐	11.22
♇	Pluto	♎	10.57
AS	I ASC	♉	25.17
MC	X MC	♒	7.41

Feminine Essence

1) I feel the most access to my feminine when I am:

_____

_____

_____

2) 3 Words that Describe my Feminine Nature:

_____

_____

3) How would a good friend, lover or partner describe my feminine side?

_____

_____

_____

MY VENUS IS IN...

SIGN   HOUSE   PHASE   VENUS STAR POINT

4 VENUS PHASES:
Reset and Morning Phases

1) RESET PHASE:

The Queen of Heaven and Earth goes backstage for a long soak in a bath, a costume change and hot date culminating in Divine Union with her Beloved. The Essence of the next journey is conceived. Our heart transitions between the completion of the 19-month journey, actively letting go of all that was created and starting a new cycle. She makes an offering of wisdom back to the Mystery. She knows that the ending contains the seed of the new beginning. She is in motion, traveling into herself to receive the next assignment.

Reset Venus is a knower of thresholds, a bridge-maker and may know how to assist during transitions of all kinds. She is a shapeshifter, one who can feel many different perspectives. Going backwards in reflections brings forth her heart wisdom. She understands how one cycle bridges to the next. She is seeding her Essence here.

2) MORNING STAR PHASE:

The Queen of Heaven begins the Heroine's Journey once she hears the call. Our heart is young, untested, bold. We engage with life and take a risk to create something, perhaps impossible from the view of our conditioning. She begins fiercely and is slowly humbled by facing challenges when things do not go as planned. We are invited to release with as much grace as possible all that stands in the way of actualizing our original creative impulse: habits, addictions, false image, internal and external sabotage. We can keep surrendering all that stands in the way of our authenticity to know more of our Essence.

Morning Star Venus is an initiator and trailblazer. She needs to try lots of ventures and make mistakes to learn. Boldness is rewarded. Discernment is learned. She can have a youthful quality about her, no matter what age. The more she risks and follows the authentic guidance of her heart, the more she shines. She is refining her Essence here.

Underworld and Evening Star Phases

3) UNDERWORLD PHASE:

The Queen of Heaven is shocked by the revelation that she must surrender more than she imagined to become more of who she is. Our hearts deepen as we face the saboteur and some part of our identity gets annihilated. We recognize the need to call our energy home within us, retreat, tuck into our cave to find stillness and hang in the deep. This is a chance to transform our relationship to the dark, the shadow, the exiled and unloved parts of ourselves. We can discover that all the light and love that we crave from others dwells within our innermost being. We can uncover the keys to regeneration.

Underworld Venus is often a healer, medicine person, therapist or shaman. She has had many Underworld experiences to learn the art of rebirth. She emerges on the other side with wisdom and inspiration to show others how to find the topside world again. She may need time to be deeply internal to function. She is not afraid of shadow places and is often navigators of the unseen realms. She is deepening her Essence here.

4) EVENING STAR PHASE:

The Queen of Heaven becomes the Queen of Heaven and Earth. She has cultivated faith during the longest night and knows the magic of Rebirth. Her personal suffering has opened her to compassion for other beings' suffering. As she rises higher and brighter, she demonstrates the depths of her knowing. Our Feminine Essence becomes more mature and socially engaged. She needs a lot of social feedback to calibrate how effectively she is sharing her wisdom. After her heart's mission has come to completion, she shines in celebration, expressing the outer quality of the light she found within her during her Underworld experience. She enjoys the ripening and then releases as much of her wisdom to the world as possible before she fades from the Sky.

Evening Star Venus can inherently understand much about the feminine principle. Her life may prepare her to share it with the world. She is often wise beyond her years. She wants to demonstrate the deep lessons of the Underworld and bring them into the light of day. She may be a teacher or work for social causes. She feels the needs and dreams of the collective. She benefits from a lot of social feedback to stay tuned to her impact on others. She is emanating her Essence here.

Houses

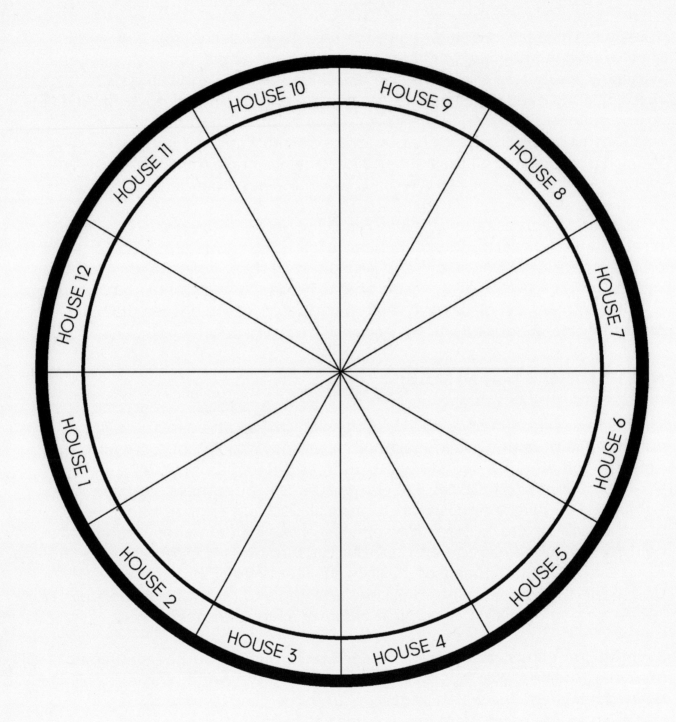

Houses

AREAS OF LIFE WHERE THE SIGNS EXPRESS THEMSELVES

1
- Individuation
- Self/Identity
- Presentation
- How others see us
- Face • Head • Body
- Health • Vitality
- Outlook on Life
- How we Assert Ourselves

2
- Inner Resources
- Possessions • Income
- Relationship to Finances • Stability in the World • Orientation to Physical World
- Self-esteem • Values
- Sensuality • How we Receive

3
- Learning • Mental Reality • Exchanging Info • Short Trips
- Communications & Connections in our Environment • Siblings or Close Friends • The Holy In the Ordinary

4
- Foundations
- Home/Family
- Earliest Awareness of Self • Roots
- Ancestry • Mother
- Conditioning • Early Childhood Imprints

5
- Self-Love • Creative and Erotic Expression
- Courtship • Art
- Creation Energy
- Experiences of Pleasure • Risk Taking
- Important Children in Our Life

6
- Physical Health
- Self-Care • Duties
- Service • Self-Control
- Vocation • Work Ethic • Employees
- How One Meets Defeat

7
- Partnerships & Allies
- Significant One-On-One Relationships : Business, Friend, Love, Therapy
- Open Enemies
- Agreements • Ability to Listen & Respond

8
- Process of Personal Transformation
- Shared Resources:
- Deepest Intimacy
- Psychic Experiences
- Loss • Taboo
- Shadow • Power
- Underworld • Loss

9
- Expanding to Create Greater Meaning
- Teachers • Big Vision
- Wisdom Traditions
- Foreign Cultures
- Long Distance Travel
- Connection to Spiritual Path

10
- Personal Power Manifest • Social Position • Career
- Contribution to Social Order
- Public Role • Ethics
- Reputation • Father Authority Figures

11
- Groups & Networks •
- Connecting Globally through Technology
- Social Circles
- Kinship with those who Share our Highest Vision • Future
- Revolutionary Ideas

12
- Relationship with Source • Collective Unconscious • Unity
- Absolute Truth
- Selfless Service
- Karma • Debts and Memories of the Past
- Legacies • Death
- The Great Beyond

VENUS WISDOM

Planets

SHOW US WHAT PART OF US IS ACTING, ASPECTS OF SELF, BASIC
PSCYCHOLOGICAL FUNCTIONS

SUN — My identity and the quality of life force that animates me, inspires me towards purpose

MOON — My emotions, conditioning, reactions, sensitivity, daily habits

MERCURY — My capacity to think, speak, learn, reason, perspective

VENUS — My ability to relate, receive, attune, connect and feel, appreciate and embody beauty, feminine nature

MARS — My capacity to act, to get what I want, assert my desire, physical energy, will, masculine nature

JUPITER — My search for meaning and truth, ability to expand to understand, blessings and luck

SATURN — My capacity to create structure, form and discipline, relationship with authority and limits

URANUS — My originality, ability to liberate myself from limitations, freedom, the unexpected

NEPTUNE — My capacity to transcend the finite self through unity with greater whole, dreams, visions, imagination

PLUTO — My capacity to transform and renew through processes of death and rebirth

CHIRON — My capacity to unconditionally love myself through realizing the medicine of my broken open heart

Signs

SHOW US HOW PLANETS ACT
12 DIFFERENT EXPRESSIONS OF CONSCIOUSNESS

ARIES
I am: fire, individuation, active, vital energy, primal urge, starter, direct, desire, impulsive, willful, impatient, quick to anger, demanding, combative

TAURUS
I have: earth, stabilizing, orienting to physical realm, productive, reliable, sensual, fertile, embodiment, possessive, stubborn, passive

GEMINI
I think: air, duality, communication, quick-minded, changeable, curious, movement, seeks to understand, rationalizing, indecisive, prone to gossip

CANCER
I feel: water, nurturing, attuned, emotional, caring, sentimental, sensitive, maternal, insecure, fearful, moody

LEO
I show: fire, creative expression, shining at center, generous, proud, self-love, seeking approval, insensitive to others

VIRGO
I analyze: earth, practical, refining, clarity, systems, attuned to natural systems, perfecting, in service, detail-oriented, critical, narrow-minded,

LIBRA
I relate: air, diplomatic, seeking to understand partnership, balance, social, loves justice, indecisive, going between extremes, co-dependent

SCORPIO
I transform: water, deep, intense feelings, shadow work, detective, authentic, regenerative, hurtful, manipulative, controlling, negative

SAGITARIUS
I seek: fire, expansion, learning through expansion, idealistic, exploring, seeking wisdom, impatient, self-righteous, deceptive

CAPRICORN
I utilize: earth, accomplishing, socially responsible, mature, structured, manifesting, contracted, cautious, depressive, controlling

AQUARIUS
I know: air, intelligence, innovative, humanitarian, rebellious, quantum leaps, passionately committed to change with detachment, impersonal

PISCES
I imagine: water, sensitive, understands unity, unconditional love, compassionate, nebulous, martyrdom, emotionally manipulative

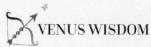
VENUS WISDOM

REFLECTIONS ON MY VENUS IN GEMINI HEROINE'S JOURNEY

• What were the themes in my life during the last Venus cycle that began on June 3, 2020, and ended on January 8th, 2022?

• Did anything memorable happen at the start of the cycle?

• What were the themes in my relationships?

• What was I healing?

• What was happening in my ability to connect, bond, care for myself, feel nourished, share love, and appreciate myself?

• What did I value most?

REFLECTIONS ON MY VENUS IN GEMINI HEROINE'S JOURNEY

• Did I have significant beginnings or endings?

• 3 positive qualities I saw in myself then were:

• Did I feel connected to my inner guidance?

• Was I expressing my truth when needed?

• What were my deepest heart longings?

• What were the most challenging qualities I was expressing?

• Which layers of personality am I no longer identifying with?

January 2022: RESET

WEEK 1: (1/3 - 1/9)

MONDAY

TUESDAY

WEDNESDAY

THURSDAY

FRIDAY

WEEKEND
NEW CYCLE BEGINS
VENUS CONJUNCT SUN
IN CAPRICORN 1/8/22 @ 18°

WEEK 2: (1/10 - 1/16)

MONDAY

TUESDAY

WEDNESDAY

THURSDAY

FRIDAY

WEEKEND

RESET PHASE REFLECTIONS

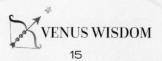

January/February 2022: MORNING STAR

WEEK 3: (1/17 - 1/23)

MONDAY

TUESDAY

WEDNESDAY

THURSDAY

FRIDAY

WEEKEND

WEEK 4: (1/24 - 1/30)

MONDAY

TUESDAY

WEDNESDAY

THURSDAY

FRIDAY

WEEKEND

February 2022: MORNING STAR

WEEK 5: (1/31 - 2/6)

MONDAY

TUESDAY

WEDNESDAY

THURSDAY

FRIDAY

WEEKEND

WEEK 6: (2/7 - 2/13)

MONDAY

TUESDAY

WEDNESDAY

THURSDAY

FRIDAY

WEEKEND

VENUS WISDOM

February 2022: MORNING STAR

WEEK 7: (2/14 - 2/20)

MONDAY

TUESDAY

WEDNESDAY

THURSDAY

FRIDAY

WEEKEND

WEEK 8: (2/21 - 2/27)

MONDAY

TUESDAY

WEDNESDAY

THURSDAY

FRIDAY

WEEKEND

March 2022: MORNING STAR

WEEK 9: (2/28 - 3/6)

MONDAY

TUESDAY

WEDNESDAY

THURSDAY

FRIDAY

WEEKEND

WEEK 10: (3/7 - 3/13)

MONDAY

TUESDAY

WEDNESDAY

THURSDAY

FRIDAY

WEEKEND

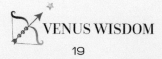
VENUS WISDOM

March 2022: MORNING STAR

WEEK 11: (3/14 - 3/20)

MONDAY

TUESDAY

WEDNESDAY

THURSDAY

FRIDAY

WEEKEND

WEEK 12: (3/21 - 3/27)

MONDAY

TUESDAY

WEDNESDAY

THURSDAY

FRIDAY

WEEKEND

March/April 2022: MORNING STAR

WEEK 13: (3/28 - 4/3)

MONDAY

TUESDAY

WEDNESDAY

THURSDAY

FRIDAY

WEEKEND

WEEK 14: (4/4 - 4/10)

MONDAY

TUESDAY

WEDNESDAY

THURSDAY

FRIDAY

WEEKEND

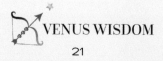

VENUS WISDOM

April 2022: MORNING STAR

WEEK 15: (4/11 - 4/17)

MONDAY

TUESDAY

WEDNESDAY

THURSDAY

FRIDAY

WEEKEND

WEEK 16: (4/18 - 4/24)

MONDAY

TUESDAY

WEDNESDAY

THURSDAY

FRIDAY

WEEKEND

April/May 2022: MORNING STAR

WEEK 17: (4/25 - 5/1)

MONDAY

TUESDAY

WEDNESDAY

THURSDAY

FRIDAY

WEEKEND

WEEK 18: (5/2 - 5/8)

MONDAY

TUESDAY

WEDNESDAY

THURSDAY

FRIDAY

WEEKEND

May 2022: MORNING STAR

WEEK 19: (5/9 - 5/15)

MONDAY

TUESDAY

WEDNESDAY

THURSDAY

FRIDAY

WEEKEND

WEEK 20: (5/16 - 5/22)

MONDAY

TUESDAY

WEDNESDAY

THURSDAY

FRIDAY

WEEKEND

May/June 2022: MORNING STAR

WEEK 21: (5/23 - 5/29)

MONDAY

TUESDAY

WEDNESDAY

THURSDAY

FRIDAY

WEEKEND

WEEK 22: (5/30 - 6/5)

MONDAY

TUESDAY

WEDNESDAY

THURSDAY

FRIDAY

WEEKEND

June 2022: MORNING STAR

WEEK 23: (6/6 - 6/12)

MONDAY

TUESDAY

WEDNESDAY

THURSDAY

FRIDAY

WEEKEND

WEEK 24: (6/13 - 6/19)

MONDAY

TUESDAY

WEDNESDAY

THURSDAY

FRIDAY

WEEKEND

VENUS WISDOM

June/July 2022: MORNING STAR

WEEK 25: (6/20 - 6/26)

MONDAY

TUESDAY

WEDNESDAY

THURSDAY

FRIDAY

WEEKEND

WEEK 26: (6/27 - 7/3)

MONDAY

TUESDAY

WEDNESDAY

THURSDAY

FRIDAY

WEEKEND

July 2022: MORNING STAR

WEEK 27: (7/4 - 7/10)

MONDAY

TUESDAY

WEDNESDAY

THURSDAY

FRIDAY

WEEKEND

WEEK 28: (7/11 - 7/17)

MONDAY

TUESDAY

WEDNESDAY

THURSDAY

FRIDAY

WEEKEND

July 2022: MORNING STAR

WEEK 29: (7/18 - 7/24)

MONDAY

TUESDAY

WEDNESDAY

THURSDAY

FRIDAY

WEEKEND

WEEK 30: (7/25 - 7/31)

MONDAY

TUESDAY

WEDNESDAY

THURSDAY

FRIDAY

WEEKEND

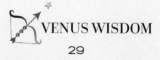

VENUS WISDOM

August 2022: MORNING STAR

WEEK 31: (8/1 - 8/7)

MONDAY

TUESDAY

WEDNESDAY

THURSDAY

FRIDAY

WEEKEND

WEEK 32: (8/8 - 8/14)

MONDAY

TUESDAY

WEDNESDAY

THURSDAY

FRIDAY

WEEKEND

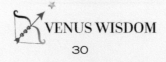

MORNING STAR REFLECTIONS

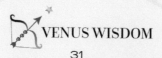

August 2022: UNDERWORLD

WEEK 1: (8/15 - 8/21)

MONDAY

TUESDAY

WEDNESDAY

THURSDAY

FRIDAY

WEEKEND

WEEK 2: (8/22 - 8/28)

MONDAY

TUESDAY

WEDNESDAY

THURSDAY

FRIDAY

WEEKEND

August & September 2022: UNDERWORLD

WEEK 3: (8/29 - 9/4)

MONDAY

TUESDAY

WEDNESDAY

THURSDAY

FRIDAY

WEEKEND

WEEK 4: (9/5 - 9/11)

MONDAY

TUESDAY

WEDNESDAY

THURSDAY

FRIDAY

WEEKEND

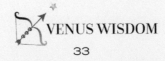

September 2022: UNDERWORLD

WEEK 5: (9/12 - 9/18)

MONDAY

TUESDAY

WEDNESDAY

THURSDAY

FRIDAY

WEEKEND

WEEK 6: (9/19 - 9/25)

MONDAY

TUESDAY

WEDNESDAY

THURSDAY

FRIDAY

WEEKEND

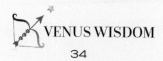

September & October 2022: UNDERWORLD

WEEK 7: (9/26 - 10/2)

MONDAY

TUESDAY

WEDNESDAY

THURSDAY

FRIDAY

WEEKEND

WEEK 8: (10/3 - 10/9)

MONDAY

TUESDAY

WEDNESDAY

THURSDAY

FRIDAY

WEEKEND

October 2022: UNDERWORLD

WEEK 9: (10/10 - 10/16)

MONDAY

TUESDAY

WEDNESDAY

THURSDAY

FRIDAY

WEEKEND

WEEK 10: (10/17 - 10/23)

MONDAY

TUESDAY

WEDNESDAY

THURSDAY

FRIDAY

WEEKEND

October & November 2022: UNDERWORLD

WEEK 11: (10/24 - 10/30)

MONDAY

TUESDAY

WEDNESDAY

THURSDAY

FRIDAY

WEEKEND

WEEK 12: (10/31 - 11/6)

MONDAY

TUESDAY

WEDNESDAY

THURSDAY

FRIDAY

WEEKEND

November 2022: UNDERWORLD

WEEK 13: (11/7 - 11/13)

MONDAY

TUESDAY

WEDNESDAY

THURSDAY

FRIDAY

WEEKEND

WEEK 14: (11/14 - 11/20)

MONDAY

TUESDAY

WEDNESDAY

THURSDAY

FRIDAY

WEEKEND

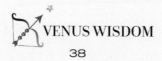

November & December 2022: UNDERWORLD

WEEK 15: (11/21 - 11/27)

MONDAY

TUESDAY

WEDNESDAY

THURSDAY

FRIDAY

WEEKEND

WEEK 16: (11/28 - 11/30)

MONDAY

TUESDAY

WEDNESDAY

UNDERWORLD REFLECTIONS

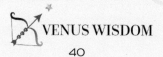

UNDERWORLD REFLECTIONS

JOIN THE VENUS WISDOM COLLECTIVE TO CONNECT WITH KEY QUESTIONS
AND FREE EVENTS TO HELP YOU SYNC WITH VENUS.
WWW.VENUSWISDOM.COM

VENUS WISDOM

December 2022: EVENING STAR

WEEK 1: (12/1 - 12/4)

THURSDAY

FRIDAY

SATURDAY

SUNDAY

WEEK 2: (12/5 - 12/11)

MONDAY

TUESDAY

WEDNESDAY

THURSDAY

FRIDAY

WEEKEND

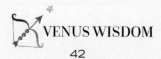

December 2022: EVENING STAR

WEEK 3: (12/12 - 12/18)

MONDAY

TUESDAY

WEDNESDAY

THURSDAY

FRIDAY

WEEKEND

WEEK 4: (12/19 - 12/25)

MONDAY

TUESDAY

WEDNESDAY

THURSDAY

FRIDAY

WEEKEND

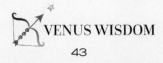

VENUS WISDOM

January 2023: EVENING STAR

WEEK 5: (12/26 - 1/1)

MONDAY

TUESDAY

WEDNESDAY

THURSDAY

FRIDAY

WEEKEND

WEEK 6: (1/2 - 1/8)

MONDAY

TUESDAY

WEDNESDAY

THURSDAY

FRIDAY

WEEKEND

January 2023: EVENING STAR

WEEK 7: (1/9 - 1/15)

MONDAY

TUESDAY

WEDNESDAY

THURSDAY

FRIDAY

WEEKEND

WEEK 8: (1/16 - 1/22)

MONDAY

TUESDAY

WEDNESDAY

THURSDAY

FRIDAY

WEEKEND

January & February 2023: EVENING STAR

WEEK 9: (1/23 - 1/29)

MONDAY

TUESDAY

WEDNESDAY

THURSDAY

FRIDAY

WEEKEND

WEEK 10: (1/30 - 2/5)

MONDAY

TUESDAY

WEDNESDAY

THURSDAY

FRIDAY

WEEKEND

February 2023: EVENING STAR

WEEK 11: (2/6 - 2/12)

MONDAY

TUESDAY

WEDNESDAY

THURSDAY

FRIDAY

WEEKEND

WEEK 12: (2/13 - 2/19)

MONDAY

TUESDAY

WEDNESDAY

THURSDAY

FRIDAY

WEEKEND

February & March 2023: EVENING STAR

WEEK 13: (2/20 - 2/26)

MONDAY

TUESDAY

WEDNESDAY

THURSDAY

FRIDAY

WEEKEND

WEEK 14: (2/27 - 3/5)

MONDAY

TUESDAY

WEDNESDAY

THURSDAY

FRIDAY

WEEKEND

March 2023: EVENING STAR

WEEK 15: (3/6 - 3/12)

MONDAY

TUESDAY

WEDNESDAY

THURSDAY

FRIDAY

WEEKEND

WEEK 16: (3/13 - 3/19)

MONDAY

TUESDAY

WEDNESDAY

THURSDAY

FRIDAY

WEEKEND

March & April 2023: EVENING STAR

WEEK 17: (3/20 - 3/26)

MONDAY

TUESDAY

WEDNESDAY

THURSDAY

FRIDAY

WEEKEND

WEEK 18: (3/27 - 4/2)

MONDAY

TUESDAY

WEDNESDAY

THURSDAY

FRIDAY

WEEKEND

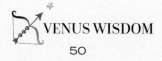

April 2023: EVENING STAR

WEEK 19: (4/3 - 4/9)

MONDAY

TUESDAY

WEDNESDAY

THURSDAY

FRIDAY

WEEKEND

WEEK 20: (4/10 - 4/16)

MONDAY

TUESDAY

WEDNESDAY

THURSDAY

FRIDAY

WEEKEND

VENUS WISDOM

April 2023: EVENING STAR

WEEK 21: (4/17 - 4/23)

MONDAY

TUESDAY

WEDNESDAY

THURSDAY

FRIDAY

WEEKEND

WEEK 22: (4/24 - 4/30)

MONDAY

TUESDAY

WEDNESDAY

THURSDAY

FRIDAY

WEEKEND

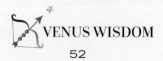
VENUS WISDOM

May 2023: EVENING STAR

WEEK 23: (5/1 - 5/7)

MONDAY

TUESDAY

WEDNESDAY

THURSDAY

FRIDAY

WEEKEND

WEEK 24: (5/8 - 5/14)

MONDAY

TUESDAY

WEDNESDAY

THURSDAY

FRIDAY

WEEKEND

May 2023: EVENING STAR

WEEK 25: (5/15 - 5/21)

MONDAY

TUESDAY

WEDNESDAY

THURSDAY

FRIDAY

WEEKEND

WEEK 26: (5/22 - 5/28)

MONDAY

TUESDAY

WEDNESDAY

THURSDAY

FRIDAY

WEEKEND

WEEK 27: (5/29 - 6/4)

MONDAY

TUESDAY

WEDNESDAY

THURSDAY

FRIDAY

WEEKEND

WEEK 28: (6/5 - 6/11)

MONDAY

TUESDAY

WEDNESDAY

THURSDAY

FRIDAY

WEEKEND

June 2023: EVENING STAR

WEEK 29: (6/12 - 6/18)

MONDAY

TUESDAY

WEDNESDAY

THURSDAY

FRIDAY

WEEKEND

WEEK 30: (6/19 - 6/25)

MONDAY

TUESDAY

WEDNESDAY

THURSDAY

FRIDAY

WEEKEND

June & July 2023: EVENING STAR

WEEK 31: (6/26 - 7/2)

MONDAY

TUESDAY

WEDNESDAY

THURSDAY

FRIDAY

WEEKEND

WEEK 32: (7/3 - 7/9)

MONDAY

TUESDAY

WEDNESDAY

THURSDAY

FRIDAY

WEEKEND

July 2023: EVENING STAR

WEEK 33: (7/10 - 7/16)

MONDAY

TUESDAY

WEDNESDAY

THURSDAY

FRIDAY

WEEKEND

WEEK 34: (7/17 - 7/23)

MONDAY

TUESDAY

WEDNESDAY

THURSDAY

FRIDAY

WEEKEND

July & August 2023: EVENING STAR

WEEK 35: (7/24 - 7/30)

MONDAY

TUESDAY

WEDNESDAY

THURSDAY

FRIDAY

WEEKEND

WEEK 36: (7/31 - 8/6)

MONDAY

TUESDAY

WEDNESDAY

THURSDAY

FRIDAY

WEEKEND

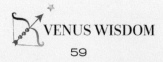

August 2023: EVENING STAR

WEEK 37: (8/7 - 8/13)

MONDAY

TUESDAY

WEDNESDAY

THURSDAY

FRIDAY

WEEKEND
8/13/23: NEW CYCLE BEGINS
VENUS CONJUNCT SUN
IN LEO @ 20°

EVENING STAR REFLECTIONS

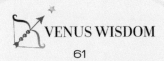

VENUS WISDOM

REFLECTIONS ON MY VENUS IN CAPRICORN HEROINE'S JOURNEY

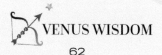

VENUS WISDOM

REFLECTIONS ON MY VENUS IN CAPRICORN HEROINE'S JOURNEY

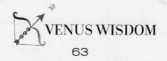

Printed in Great Britain
by Amazon

17406868R10036